"Mush-hole"
Memories of a Residential School

as told by
Maddie Harper

Art by
Carlos Freire

Sister Vision

Black Women and Women of Colour Press

This book was produced by the collective effort of The Turtle Island Publication Group
and Sister Vision Press.

Canadian Cataloguing in Publication Data
Harper, Maddie
Residential schools
ISBN 0-920813-98-4

1.Harper, Maddie – Juvenile literature.
2. Indians of North America – Canada – Residential schools – Juvenile literature.*
3. Indians of North America – Canada – Women – Biography – Juvenile literature.
I. Freire, Carlos, 1943 - II. Title
E96.5.H37 1993   j371.97'9702   C94-930222-8

*Published with the kind assistance of the Canada Council
and the Ontario Arts Council*

Published by
Sister Vision Press
P.O. Box 217, Station E,
Toronto, Ontario,
Canada, M6H 4E2

I think it was about 1914 when they started taking the children to residential schools. I was born on a reserve and I really didn't know the reasons why I was put into a residential school. I only remember that, at age seven, I was in an institution with about 200 other little girls like myself and when I reflect back on it now, it is very emotional for me. Now I can talk about it.

We were told what time to get up, what time to eat, when to pray and when to go to the bathroom. Everything was time; everything was regulated, and I realize that during that process they had stolen my will . . . my will to do anything and my freedom of choice in all matters. If we didn't do what we were told they'd take you to the principal's office and they'd pull down your pants and give it to you on your bare ass.

Also during the process, we weren't allowed to speak our language and we were taught nothing about our traditional ways, or our heritage or anything about our culture. The residential school I was in, the Brantford School, was called the "mush-hole" because we were given mush every morning.

I spent eight years in the school and had little contact with anyone from the outside world because my mother had passed away. I only had my Dad left. When I became a young woman I got to meet some of my other family members.

I think one of the greatest impacts I felt was the influence of the church during my upbringing because it was drilled into us – the teachings of the bible, the prayers and the hymns. So, we learned to know our boundaries and we knew that we had to adhere because what alternative did we have? Perhaps to try and run away, which I attempted to do several times and finally was successful when I was about fifteen years old.

After I escaped from the school, I was very confused and I went back to the reserve where I was born, to be with my family and then I realized that the place was an alien place for me. I was institutionalized for so long.

There were a lot of things that were bothering me inside. Things I had learned in school like being educated and having a good job. Getting married and having a nice family with children. But I was confused and not feeling good about who I was.

I used to see a lot of native people around, but I didn't really know anybody except for a couple of friends I had met at school. I spent time with them.

My feeling confused and not very good about myself happens to many native people and we turn to alcohol. I had seen it on the reserve and that was my justification.

I started drinking and made a career out of it for a few years and it got me into a lot of trouble, but I think now that drinking is where I found my escape. I didn't have anywhere else to turn and I wasn't fortunate enough to be able to go to Elders, like we have today.

I tried several times to straighten up, but all the time I was trying to straighten up, and feel good about who I was, the thing that kept coming up in the back of my mind was God, the God that I was taught to believe in, back in residential school. I went back to the church to try and find myself.

The church was good for me with the fellowship, but it really didn't give me everything I was looking for because I still felt empty inside about being a native person. Later on, I was fortunate enough to run into some Elders who taught the native way of life and ceremonies and traditional ways that I had never, ever heard in my life. I immediately went to them and talked with them about the ways of the Creator that I hadn't known anything about. That was the beginning of the native way of life for me, which was probably about 1980.

The purpose of the whole [institution] thing, was to assimilate us. It was to take our identity away from us, because, after all, we were pagans. Well, today, I am a born-again pagan and I'm proud to say that. I look at life as a learning process and I'm going to be learning for the rest of my life, but I've had a lot of experience.

What has happened historically has not worked for us and that is why we have to teach our own people and give up ourselves for others to learn. That was how I learned who I was – through someone else who gave my identity back to me. To know where my roots were, to know what my heritage was, because up to that point when I learned about these things, all of that was ignored through the educational system.

People have to understand that we have a very sacred and good way, our native way and the Creator gave us this way to practise. Now I carry these messages to the people in Central and South America because I've travelled down there and listened to other traditional people, indigenous people, of that area.

Today, it is like I left my old life behind because I went through so much pain and had to endure so many hardships. I have different concepts to implement with my family. We have more freedom of speech and we do things in a more caring and sharing way, with a circle. We learn and teach our children the real stories about Christmas and about Christopher Columbus so that they can understand that they have choices and so that they can feel good about themselves.

My husband says we have to do our work as aboriginal people, but we also wish and want to cooperate with those people who want to help us and who want to understand and work in solidarity with us.

Other books in this series by the
Turtle Island Publication Group are:

The Seven Fires: An Ojibway Prophecy

as told by Sally Gaikesheyongai

Onkwehonwe-Neha: Our Ways

as told by

Skonaganleh:ra (Sylvia Maracle)

Other books by First Nations women published by Sister Vision Press

Bird Talk/Bineshiinh Dibaajmowin
by Lenore Keeshig Tobias, illustrated by
Polly Keeshig- Tobais

Beneath the Naked Sun, poetry by Connie Fife

The Invitation, a novel by Cyndy Baskin

*The Colour of Resistance: A Collection of
Contemporary Writing by Aboriginal Women*
anthologised by Connie Fife